Princess Evie

For Pip & Jess xx
Sarah KilBride

To Agnieszka
Sophie Tilley

SIMON AND SCHUSTER
First published in Great Britain in 2014 by Simon and Schuster UK Ltd
1st Floor, 222 Gray's Inn Road, London WC1X 8HB
A CBS Company
Text copyright © 2014 Sarah KilBride
Illustrations based on artwork originated by Sophie Tilley © 2014
Concept © 2009 Simon and Schuster UK
The right of Sarah KilBride and Sophie Tilley to be identified
as the author and illustrator of this work has been asserted by them
in accordance with the Copyright, Designs and Patents Act, 1988
All rights reserved, including the right of reproduction in whole or in part in any form
A CIP catalogue record for this book is available from the British Library upon request
PB ISBN: 978-1-4711-2178-4
eBook ISBN: 978-1-4711-2179-1
Printed and bound by CPI Group (UK) Ltd, Croydon, CR0 4YY
1 3 5 7 9 10 8 6 4 2

Princess Evie

Sarah KilBride
Sophie Tilley

Unicorn Riding Camp

SIMON AND SCHUSTER

CHAPTER 1

Sleepy Head

"What a perfect day, Diamond!" said Princess Evie, as she trotted through the gates of Starlight Stables.

Even though it was early, the sun was scorching. It was much hotter in the stable yard than on the top of the Golden Mountain, where they had enjoyed a lovely cool breeze. The bright morning sun made Evie's Connemara pony's coat gleam.

"I think your friends are pleased to see you, Diamond!"

Evie was right. All her lovely ponies

were trotting to the gate, neighing,
squealing and welcoming Diamond
back.

It wasn't only Evie's ponies that were
glad to see them. Evie's little kitten
Sparkles skipped over to the tie post
and rubbed against Evie's ankle.

"We've just had the most amazing ride," smiled Evie. "The Golden Mountain is ever so high. At first we were surrounded by mountain clouds, but they soon cleared and then we could see for miles."

Diamond was the perfect pony for mountain rides. She had great stamina and was very strong. Of course Evie loved riding all of her ponies, especially on summer days like these. But Evie's ponies weren't any old ponies. They were magic ponies. Whenever Evie rode them through the tunnel of trees, they took her on magical adventures in faraway lands.

Evie's ponies were transformed the moment they came out of the tunnel. For instance, when Neptune galloped out onto a beach her coat became the colour of the sparkling ocean. And that wasn't the only magic that happened – Evie's clothes changed too! She loved the beautiful new outfits she wore on their adventures. When she went to the North Pole with the snow fairies, she wore a gorgeous fluffy pink cloak and warm boots. Evie looked up at the cloudless sky – it was hard to imagine snow today!

She checked to see if Diamond had cooled down, especially where the saddle had been and under her pony's elbows and hind legs. Because Diamond's breathing had slowed down to normal Evie could now give her some fresh water and brush out her shining coat.

"You've worked hard this morning,
Diamond, climbing up that steep
mountain and galloping along the
ridge."

Evie went into the tack room to get
her grooming kit and Sparkles padded
in after her. It wasn't just Diamond
who was hot. Evie had been out in the
sun for quite some time and the tack
room felt lovely and cool. The walls

were lined with saddles, bridles and, of course, rosettes. Evie walked towards the metal trunk where she kept her grooming kit. As her eyes adjusted to the shadows of the tack room, she noticed something.

"Have we had visitors this morning, Sparkles?"

Sparkles miaowed. Of course, he couldn't talk – he was only a cat, but Evie was positive that he could understand every word she said.

"I think someone's been here while I was out on the mountain. Look!"

Evie pointed to the metal trunk and Sparkles hopped up for a closer inspection.

There, leaning against a bottle of hoof oil, was a golden envelope.

"Who's it from?" asked Evie.

Sparkles sniffed the envelope, and then looked at Evie, blinking patiently.

"You're right – there's only one way to find out!"

Evie picked the envelope up and took out the letter. As she read it, she smiled.

"Come on, Sparkles, I have to read this to Diamond!" And they raced out, to the sunny yard with the letter.

To
Princess
Evie

Dear Evie,

How are things at Starlight Stables? I hope you're enjoying this lovely summer with all of your gorgeous ponies – fantastic riding weather, isn't it?

I'm writing to you because I wondered if you and Diamond would like to come to the Cloud Kingdom and join our Unicorn Riding Camp. It starts today and should be great fun. There'll be lots of cloud sprites there and they'll be loads of lessons and activities to help us learn all about our unicorns. Just leave your kit in the stable yard and I'll send a cloud to pick it up. I'll be waiting for you on the clouds when you come out of the tunnel of trees.

Really hope you can make it – it would be brilliant to see you and Diamond again.

Lots of love,

Skye xxxxxx

PS: PLEASE bring Sparkles too xxxxxxx

PPS: Please give all your ponies a hug from me.

PPPS: PLEASE give Sparkles an extra-special hug too!!!!

Diamond neighed. She loved taking Evie away on adventures and Unicorn Riding Camp certainly sounded very exciting. Diamond and Evie had shared an amazing adventure the last time they'd visited the Cloud Kingdom. They had competed in the Unicorn Games and had even won first prize in the obstacle race!

There was no time to lose, Evie raced into the tack room to pack. She found the special riding gloves that Skye had given her, embroidered with little gold unicorns. Then she checked her grooming kit, making sure that everything was clean and in good condition.

"How thrilling – we're going to see Skye and her magic unicorn Jewel again," said Evie as she took her rucksack of useful things down from its peg. "I can't wait!"

She carried her kit out into the yard.

"Skye said to leave our kit here," said Evie, "I wonder if that's the cloud that's going to take it to the Cloud Kingdom?"

The blue sky had been clear a moment ago but now there was a large white cloud floating over the Golden Mountain. As it came towards Starlight Castle it floated lower and lower, drifting past the turrets, and over the gardens. By the time it arrived at Starlight Stables it was skimming along the ground.

Sparkles jumped up into Evie's arms – he'd never seen anything quite like this before! The cloud came towards them and for a few seconds they couldn't see a thing, then it floated back up into the sky.

"Look at that!" said Evie.

There was just an empty space where her kit box had been.

"Hop up Sparkles, it's time to go to the Cloud Kingdom!" said Evie as she put on her rucksack of useful things. "I think our luggage will be there before us!"

Evie and Sparkles mounted Diamond and soon they were galloping towards the tunnel of trees. Evie closed her eyes and took a deep breath.

CHAPTER 2

Away to
Unicorn Stables

When Evie opened her eyes the
Cloud Kingdom stretched out around
them for miles. The sunshine made
the clouds glitter with pretty pastel
colours. Diamond's coat shimmered
with the same soft colours and she now
had a magnificent golden unicorn's
horn that sparkled in the sunshine.
Evie looked down and saw that she
was wearing a smart riding jacket

embroidered with fine gold thread, a
pair of jodhpurs and gleaming riding
boots.

"I think we're ready for Unicorn Camp," she whispered, as they trotted out onto the soft, fluffy clouds.

"You certainly are!" called a friendly voice.

It was Skye. The cloud sprite appeared from the shimmering mist on her beautiful unicorn, Jewel. Her pretty

waistcoat was edged with daisies and her pale pink jodhpurs were decorated with silver thread.

"Skye!" laughed Evie. "How lovely to see you."

Jewel whinnied and Diamond and Jewel touched noses and said their unicorn hellos.

"I'm so pleased you could make it, Evie," said Skye.

"We wouldn't have missed Unicorn Riding Camp for the world!" said Evie.

"Are you ready for a gallop, Diamond?" asked Skye.

Diamond neighed and tossed her sparkling mane.

"Follow me, Evie! We'll be there in no time," said Skye.

Skye turned her unicorn around and broke into a fast trot, a canter and then a gallop. Diamond didn't need any encouragement to follow and soon they were racing along the clouds. Evie could feel her cheeks glow as the wind whistled past.

They sped through puffy white clouds

that splashed the girls with rainbow
drops. They sailed over great powdery
plains and jumped across small pink
clouds that patterned the sky like
stepping stones.

Normally when Diamond galloped
Evie could hear her pony's hooves on
the ground, but Diamond was galloping

along silently with her glittering mane flying. Evie remembered that a unicorn's hooves never make a sound – it was one of the magical things about them.

Skye was right, it wasn't long before they were at the gates of the riding school in the clouds.

"This is where they train the Unicorn Olympic Team," said Skye excitedly. "I've always dreamt about riding here."

The friends dismounted, landing softly. Evie thought that walking on clouds felt a little like walking on snow. Her feet gently sank, leaving little prints. Skye opened the beautiful golden gate.

"We'll take our unicorns to the stables first and get them settled in," she said. "Then it'll be time to go to the Great Hall to meet the instructors."

As they led their unicorns into the yard they spotted a map pinned onto a post. A little cloud sprite was looking at it. She turned and called over to the friends.

"What are your unicorns' names?"

"My unicorn is called Diamond," replied Evie. "And this is Jewel."

"You're in stables eleven and twelve and we're in stable thirteen." She smiled at her unicorn. "Unlucky for some!"

She turned to take her unicorn to the stable block when two other cloud sprites arrived and trotted silently across the yard on their unicorns, almost knocking her down.

"Watch where you're going!" shouted one rider, who had a long golden plait.

The little cloud sprite was too stunned to say anything. The riders smirked at her as she stood with her mouth open.

"You'll catch flies if you stay like that!" said the rider with the long plait.

She checked the map and the other rider giggled.

"Come on, let's go and make

ourselves at home," said the first rider.
"We're in stables fourteen and fifteen."

They trotted off to find their stables.

"They're going to be our
neighbours," the little sprite said to
her unicorn. "I told you thirteen was
unlucky for some."

"Are you all right?" asked Evie.
Tears had begun to well up in the
little sprite's eyes.

"I'm fine."

"I'm sorry – we should have stuck up
for you," said Evie.

"It's a good job you didn't," said the sprite, looking down at her scuffed riding boots. "They're the Sunshine Girls and you don't want to get on the wrong side of them. I met them at last year's camp. It's best to keep out of their way."

The little cloud sprite turned and led her unicorn away.

"What's your name?" Skye called after her but she had already disappeared around the corner, taking her unicorn to her stable.

"Let's have a look at the list," said Evie, as she scanned the map. "Here we are. She's called Wanda and her unicorn is Zephyr. I wonder if she has any friends at the camp."

"Well, I think we should be her friends. That's what camp is all about," said Skye. "Let's keep an eye on her and make sure that the Sunshine Girls don't try picking on her again."

Evie and Skye led Diamond and Jewel to their stables where their grooming kits were waiting for them.

"I told you they'd be here before us, Diamond!" said Evie.

"We're opposite Wanda," smiled Skye.

"And the Sunshine Girls," added Evie. The riders who had just been so rude to Wanda were now busily settling their unicorns in. They were making quite a lot of noise about it – singing and shouting, shrieking with laughter and chasing each other about.

"They look like they're having fun," said Evie as she gently put her hand on Diamond's muzzle.

She could feel her unicorn getting
twitchy and knew that Diamond didn't
like all this noise.

"Let's get our unicorns settled," said
Skye. "We need to be in the Great Hall
for the introduction to camp in half an
hour. If we team up with Wanda we'll
get it done quickly."

So Evie and Skye went to Wanda's stable and introduced themselves. Soon they were busy helping each other.

Wanda collected some golden apples from the barrel in the yard, while Skye filled three buckets with fresh water. Evie and Sparkles went to the barn to collect some straw for their unicorns' bedding. They needed a whole bale, but the bales were too heavy for her to pick up on her own.

"Do you need a hand?" asked a kind voice.

Evie turned around. Standing behind her was the most beautiful cloud sprite she had ever seen. Light seemed to shine from her sky-blue eyes and soft curls floated around her face. She wore a pair of pale blue jodhpurs and her silk shirt had tiny pearl buttons.

"Come on," she said with a smile.
"Let's go and find a wheelbarrow."

As they lifted the bale into an old
wheelbarrow, Evie found out that
the beautiful cloud sprite's name was
Raphaela Plume and she was one of the
camp's instructors.

"I used to come to Unicorn Camp when I was younger," said Raphaela. "I hope you have as much fun as I did!"

Evie smiled, then she remembered the Sunshine Girls. She hoped they weren't going to spoil things.

The wheelbarrow wobbled all over the place and by the time they got back to the stable Raphaela and Evie were giggling.

Evie introduced her new friend to Skye and Wanda, but the cloud sprites didn't say hello or even smile. They just went red!

"See you at the meeting!" said Raphaela.

She waved and headed off towards the Great Hall. Wanda and Skye stared after her, speechless. Even the Sunshine

Girls had stopped messing about and were staring at the lovely sprite as she disappeared around the corner.

"I don't believe it!" gasped Skye. "Raphaela Plume – the most famous unicorn gold medallist in the Cloud Kingdom."

"She was chatting and laughing with you, Evie, like a normal sprite!" said Wanda.

"Well, she is normal," said Evie. "Not like you two – staring at her and not saying a word!"

"You don't understand Evie," said Wanda. "She is the most fabulous unicorn rider in the entire Cloud Kingdom!"

"I hope she's going to teach us some of her riding secrets," said Skye. "Oh, this is going to be such an amazing camp!"

She did an excited little jump into the air.

"Come on you two, before you get any giddier!" said Evie, as she picked Sparkles up. "We've got five minutes to get to the Great Hall for our meeting."

CHAPTER 3
Unicorn Camp Chaos

The Great Hall was on an enormous cloud. Sparkles led the way along the path that followed the soft curves of the cloud. As they climbed the steps, the hall's magnificent door magically opened.

"Look at that!" Evie gasped.

She pointed to the domed ceiling. It was painted with a beautiful skyscape of shimmering clouds. On one side of the dome, the morning sunrise was painted in warm colours. The evening

sky was on the opposite side. It was a
deep blue that looked as if it went on
forever, scattered with constellations of
gold stars. The arched windows were
open and pale blue curtains floated
gently in the breeze.

A little crowd of sprites was already waiting and the air was full of chattering and laughter. Clouds the size of plates floated from sprite to sprite, carrying tasty marshmallows, pink candyfloss on cocktail sticks and tiny fairy cakes that were so fluffy they almost floated away! Whenever a plate began to look empty, it magically filled up with more treats.

Skye and Wanda met a few sprites they knew and Evie recognised Rosy from when she, Diamond and Sparkles had taken part in the Unicorn Games. Rosy smiled and waved as she came over to say hello. Then the huge wooden doors at the end of the hall opened and in walked three important looking cloud sprites.

"The instructors," whispered Skye. "Look! There's Raphaela."

"I hope we don't get Professor Nimbus first," said Wanda. "She's the one on the end. She trains riders for the Olympic team."

Evie could feel poor Sparkles jump when the professor began to speak.

"Welcome to this year's Unicorn Riding Camp," said Professor Nimbus. "I hope all your unicorns have settled in. This afternoon, I will be taking the training session on riding technique."

"I am Madam Mariposa," said the older, shorter sprite who was standing beside the Professor. She had a warm smile and fluffy white hair that had silver lining like a halo. "I will be helping you learn about unicorn well-being and stable management."

"And I'm going to be helping you bond with your unicorns," said Raphaela. "And together, we will develop your unicorn empathy skills."

There was a ripple of excitement

among the cloud sprites.

"There will be a list of the groups on the noticeboard after lunch," said Professor Nimbus.

Evie spotted Professor Nimbus wink at the girl with the long blonde plait before turning to leave.

"That's Professor Nimbus' niece," Rosy whispered in her ear. "Her name's Storm."

All the cloud sprites filed out of the Great Hall and followed the long corridor to the dining room.

The dining room was hung with paintings of unicorns and each of the round tables was lit with a golden candelabra. Everyone was hungry; it had been a long morning and the room buzzed with anticipation. Wanda, Skye

and Evie shared a table and enjoyed
the fluffy bread and hot soup. Pudding
was the most delicious cake Evie had
ever tasted – layers of light sponge
with heavenly mousse in between.

"Imagine learning how to
communicate with your unicorn like
Raphaela does!" said Wanda when they
had all finished their lunch. Everyone

was starting to leave the dining room
to have a look at the list that had been
pinned on to the noticeboard.

"Stuff and nonsense!" snorted
Storm, as she and her friend pushed
past Wanda's chair. "My aunt says
the only way to communicate with a
unicorn is to show it who is the boss."

"Let's hope we're not in Storm's

group," said Wanda, and all the friends nodded.

"There's only one way to find out," said Evie. "Come on, let's go and have a look at the lists."

"Oh, this is so exciting," said Skye. "I hope we're all in the same group."

But they weren't. Skye had been put in Rosy's group.

"What a shame I'm not with you," said Skye.

PRINCESS EVIE
& DIAMOND

WANDA
& ZEPHYR

STORM
& MISTY

JUNO
& CHERUB

"It might have been a lucky escape, Skye," said Evie. "Look who's in our group."

Princess Evie & Diamond

Wanda & Zephyr

Storm & Misty

Juno & Cherub

"The Sunshine Girls," said Wanda.

"Never mind," said Skye. "They're probably lovely, once you get to know them."

"Well, there's one good thing," said Evie, seeing that Wanda was looking a little worried. "Our first lesson is with Raphaela in the arena."

"Lucky you," said Skye, "I'm with Professor Nimbus."

The friends went off to saddle up their unicorns for the first lesson. But when they reached the stable yard, they were met with complete chaos. Cloud sprites were running about and shouting, trying to catch a unicorn that had escaped from its stable. She was rearing like a wild animal. When the unicorn was finally cornered by the sprites the friends saw it was Zephyr – Wanda's unicorn.

"Zephyr!" shouted Wanda.

As soon as she heard Wanda's voice, Zephyr neighed, looking wildly around the yard for her owner.

"That animal is out of control!" said Storm, just as the instructors appeared. "Look at this mess."

"What's made Zephie do this?" asked Wanda, completely baffled by the scene of devastation.

The barrel of apples had been kicked

over, straw was strewn across the yard, water buckets had been knocked over and some tack and grooming kit lay in the big puddles.

"This is not acceptable," said Professor Nimbus, looking around the yard. "You will not join in any activities, Wanda, until you have cleaned this up. Is that clear?"

As the Professor was talking, Raphaela walked carefully towards Zephyr, murmuring quietly to the frightened unicorn. She helped Wanda put a halter on Zephyr and tied the unicorn up.

"Come along everyone, tack up, time for your first lesson," continued the Professor.

As the other sprites tacked up, Wanda, Evie and Skye looked at each other.

"There's no way you can be late for Professor Nimbus' lesson, Skye, she'll be cross." said Evie. "I'll help Wanda clear this up."

"I don't understand," said Wanda, looking at the stable door hanging off its hinges. "Zephyr has never done anything like this before. Why would she kick her door down?"

Evie and Wanda set about sweeping and cleaning the yard. Sparkles tried to cheer Wanda up by chasing after apples and catching straw that was blowing in the breeze. But the little sprite found it hard to smile.

"I just can't understand what got into Zephyr," she said.

CHAPTER 4
Raphaela's Magic

Wanda and Evie worked together to clear all the mess, and were only ten minutes late for the start of their lesson. Storm and Juno were standing by their unicorns listening to Raphaela, who was resting her hand gently on her magnificent unicorn, Galaxy.

"Hey sprites! I'm just giving a quick history of unicorns," said Raphaela. "The important thing to remember is, if you want your unicorn's trust, you must make them feel safe. When they

feel safe with you, they can relax and
will let you lead – and that's when the
magic begins!

"Our first exercise will help you get
in tune with your unicorn. Every neigh,
whinny and squeal has a meaning and,
the more you listen, the more you'll
begin to understand. It all starts with
the breath. Listen to your unicorn and

copy her breathing."

The sprites and Evie stood closely by their unicorns. In a few moments, Evie and Diamond were almost touching noses and Wanda and Zephyr were leaning shoulder to shoulder. Juno and her unicorn were nodding heads in unison, with Juno giggling and Cherub whickering.

"It's great to see you share the same sense of humour, Juno!" said Raphaela.

"OW!" yelped Storm. "Stop that now!"

Misty had been resting her head over Storm's shoulder and had started to nibble her smart riding jacket.

"Hold on, Storm."

Raphaela and Galaxy raced over to them. "She was telling you that she's your friend."

"Ruining my jacket more like," said Storm. "That's disgusting, Misty!"

Misty whinnied and shook her mane.

"Careful Storm, that's not the way to speak to your unicorn," said Raphaela. "She's grooming you like a mother does to comfort her foal."

"I don't need to be comforted," snapped Storm.

"Well," replied Raphaela, "it seems your unicorn believes that you do."

Storm looked angry and turned away.

The next part of the lesson was what everyone had been looking forward to – developing unicorn empathy skills.

"Practise this on your unicorn and, one day, you'll be able to calm and ride any unicorn in the Cloud Kingdom," Raphaela said.

"Stand close to your unicorn's midpoint. The midpoint is just by the withers, in front of your saddles. Stand quietly and try to feel your unicorn's beat. It's a cross between a pulse and a heartbeat," said Raphaela. "Let them feel your beat too."

Evie could feel Diamond's beat pulsing quietly and steadily. Diamond was standing so still and alert, Evie was sure that her unicorn was listening to hers. Next, Raphaela told the sprites to rest their arms over their unicorn's withers.

"Apply pressure so your unicorn

understands what's going to happen next," she said. "Once they steady themselves, it's time to hop up."

Everyone copied Raphaela as she demonstrated on her unicorn, Galaxy, and soon they were all up in the saddle. Everyone, that is, apart from Storm. Misty was still shifting her weight and hadn't yet settled but, instead of steadying her with the weight of her arm, Storm was pulling hard on her reins. This was making her unicorn raise her head and try to move away.

Raphaela rode over to Storm and let her unicorn gently breathe onto Misty's muzzle. The little unicorn relaxed and Storm was able to get up into the saddle.

The next task was to ride with
loose reins. "I want you to practise
going from a halt to a walk to a trot,"
said Raphaela. "Direct your unicorn
by visualising what you want her to
do and where you want to go, and
remember to talk to her."

The unicorns and their riders moved
around the space. Soon, Wanda and

Zephyr were weaving in and out of some rainbow cones. Juno giggled as Cherub began to trot after a little cloud that had floated into the arena.

"Excellent Juno, Cherub can sense that you like to play," said Raphaela.

Evie was amazed at how Diamond seemed to be able to read her mind. All she had to do was look in the direction she wanted to go, visualise turning and Diamond would take the turn.

"This is such fun!" said Wanda laughing, as Zephyr jumped over a row of little sunbeams.

"How much longer?" asked Storm, "I can't wait till our next lesson so we can start learning useful stuff."

Her unicorn was standing by a rainbow jump and wouldn't budge.

"Try not to get angry," said Raphaela, as Storm started to use her heels to try to make her unicorn move. "Perhaps it's time for a break – we've all been working hard."

Raphaela was giving Storm the chance to dismount and calm down but Storm took no notice.

"Come on!" Storm shouted. "Move it!"

She smacked Misty's hindquarters and everyone gasped. Misty reared up high on her hind legs and let out a piercing neigh that made the other unicorns jump. Her nostrils flared and the whites of her eyes flashed wildly. Before anyone could take hold of Misty, she bolted over the arena's high fence and disappeared into a cloud.

Everyone watched in amazement and the air filled with squeals of panic from the unicorns.

The unicorns and their riders all knew the danger Storm was in, as Misty took her into the Cloud Kingdom, angry and frightened. "What on earth is going here?" demanded Professor Nimbus, bursting into the arena.

Evie and the sprites looked at Raphaela. No one wanted to be the one to tell the angry Professor what had happened to her niece. Raphaela looked uncomfortable, but she managed to explain.

"My niece is in terrible danger," said the Professor. "The clouds are beginning to separate and a storm is brewing. How on earth could you have let this happen? That unicorn of hers doesn't need empathy, it needs discipline."

"Now isn't the time to discuss our differences," said Raphaela. "Our unicorns have a connection with Misty. I'll lead the group to find their friend and bring Storm back to safety."

"The Cloud Kingdom is a dangerous place. If we hear nothing from you within the hour, then I'll have no choice but to contact the Rainbow Rescue Team and tell them you have lost my niece."

The unicorns moved close together,

their noses almost touching. The
riders waited, feeling the beats of their
unicorns racing. Then the unicorns
began to whicker – little noises that
shivered out on their breath.

"They're talking," whispered Wanda.

"They're going to call to Misty," said Raphaela. "I hope that she can hear her friends."

Diamond raised her head, her unicorn horn glittering in the sun. She let out a neigh that Evie had never heard before. Evie could feel it travel through Diamond's body starting at the top of her range. As it spiralled down, the other unicorns in the circle joined in.

The unicorns' call seemed to go on for minutes, and as it went down to the lowest notes, all the unicorns at the camp had joined in. When it ended, everyone listened.

After a minute, out of the blue, came the sound everyone had been waiting for. It was Misty's reply, but it was coming from far, far away.

The unicorns pawed the ground, their ears forward, their horns glittering and their eyes searching the horizon of clouds. Together, with their riders holding on tightly, they galloped out of the arena, through the yard and the golden gate and onto the vast blanket of clouds.

"Slow down everyone, the clouds are beginning to thin," said Raphaela.

She was right, little gaps were beginning to appear as some of the cloud began to float away. Evie could see glimpses of what lay beneath and felt Sparkles snuggling up close to her to be safe. If any of the unicorns lost their footing, it would be a long way down!

CHAPTER 5
The Rescue Party

Raphaela led them carefully in single
file, scanning the clouds and making
sure they rode a safe path. They kept
their distance from any thinning clouds
and when they heard Misty neigh
again, it was a little closer.

"Hooray!" said Juno, "we're on the
right track."

"I hope Storm has managed to stay
on," said Evie.

"She doesn't seem to get on very well
with her unicorn," said Wanda.

"Storm has never been happy

with Misty," said Juno. "She always thinks other sprites' rides are better than hers." Juno turned and looked apologetically at Wanda. "She wanted Zephyr and thought that, if she made your unicorn look wild, you might want to get rid of her."

Everyone looked shocked. They all knew that a unicorn was for life.

"Get rid of Zephyr!" gasped Wanda.

"Was it Storm that broke Zephyr's door?" asked Raphaela.

"Yes," said Juno in a small voice.

"I knew Zephyr couldn't have done it." Wanda placed her hand on her unicorn's neck and pressed gently. "I never doubted you, Zephyr. I knew it wasn't you."

"You were with Storm when she turned this unicorn out of her stable

and made that mess," said Raphaela.
"Why would you stand by when she
was being so cruel?"

"She's my friend," she said. "I know
she was doing the wrong thing, but I
feel sorry for her. She's been having a
tough time."

"Being sorry for a friend who doesn't
know any better isn't enough," said
Raphaela. "You need to be strong and

help Storm to do the right thing, even if that means risking losing her as a friend."

The procession fell silent. The clouds were darkening and a mist was beginning to form on the clouds.

"Will the unicorns know their way back?" asked Juno.

"Only when the mist and the storm have cleared," said Raphaela.

"That might take longer than an hour," said Wanda, remembering Professor Nimbus's was going to call the Rainbow Rescue Team.

Everyone knew that if they weren't back within an hour, Raphaela would be in a lot of trouble.

"We don't want to get caught in the storm," said Juno.

"Let me see if I've got anything

that might help," said Evie. "I'm sure there's a compass in here."

She opened her rucksack of useful things and, while she was looking, pulled out a pencil and a ball of red string. The instant Sparkles saw the string he started to unravel it with his paws.

"You're brilliant, Sparkles!" said Evie. "We'll leave a trail of string and follow it on our way back."

Everyone felt better knowing they would be able to get back safely. They had travelled a long way from the Unicorn Riding School and no one wanted to get caught in a cloud storm.

"What's that?" whispered Raphaela.

Everyone stopped and listened.

"Help!"

It was Storm shouting.

The search party hurried through the mist, following her calls. And there they were, Storm and Misty, stranded on an island of cloud. Evie could see the gap between them their cloud and Storm's was widening. Storm was looking pale and Evie could see that Misty was trembling, they were both petrified.

"Help!" shouted Storm. "Help me!"

"The only one who can help you is

your unicorn," called over Raphaela.
"Stay calm and try to remember what
you learnt this morning."

The only way Storm was going to
be able to get off the cloud was if her
unicorn could jump over the gap.

"Misty is a good jumper, Storm,"
called Juno. "Remember when she won
the rainbow jumping at the Unicorn

Games? She can jump that gap easily."

Storm and Misty's cloud was floating further away. If Misty was going to jump, she would have to do it quickly.

"Calm your unicorn with your breathing and soothe her with your words," Raphaela shouted across to Storm. "She has to trust you and feel safe."

Storm walked steadily to her unicorn's midpoint.

"Good girl, we'll be all right, just you see," Storm was breathing slowly.

The unicorns, Evie, Sparkles and all the sprites watched as Storm tried to calm her unicorn. Their little cloud island drifted away a bit more and Evie could see the huge drop below. It made her feel dizzy. Evie knew she'd be terrified if she had to take this jump.

Storm mounted Misty and Evie was amazed to see, for the first time, they looked like a riding pair.

"Well done, Storm," called Raphaela. "Now take your time and try to visualise Misty soaring through the air and landing safely, just like we did in the arena."

The pair stood still, and Storm

closed her eyes. When she opened them, Misty began to paw at the ground as if she couldn't wait, her eyes sparkling and her golden horn gleaming. The little unicorn reared up proudly and then began a fierce gallop towards the edge of the cloud.

They only had a short run up before jumping. No one dared to breathe as the little unicorn flew into the air.

She sailed over the gap and landed silently not far from Evie, Sparkles and Diamond.

Everyone cheered and whooped and neighed, the sound echoed through the clouds for miles around. "Thank you for saving us," said Storm, as she leant over to Raphaela and hugged her.

"It was you and your brave unicorn that did all the hard work," said

Raphaela. "I'm very proud of you."

"I'm very proud of Misty," said Storm, giving her unicorn a gentle hug. "I've been so hard on her. No wonder she wanted to run away from me!"

"I think she's seen another side to you," said Evie. "We all have."

Storm's face changed and her smile disappeared.

"There's something that I need to tell you, Wanda," she said, "about what happened in the yard after lunch."

"You can talk while we make our way back," said Raphaela. "We have to follow the red string and find our way to the stables quickly."

"Before the storm starts," said Evie, looking at the dark clouds that had begun to hiss and spit.

Poor Sparkles hid under Evie's

jacket! He hated thunder and could feel in his whiskers that the storm was about to start.

CHAPTER 6
Home and Dry

The unicorns followed the trail of red string, walking nose to tail through the crackling fog and storm clouds. Underneath their silent hooves the dark clouds rumbled. The cloudscape was changing fast. When they came to the end of the red string, Evie searched the horizon but the Unicorn Stables were nowhere to be seen.

After a few seconds, the sound of neighing filled the air.

"It's the other unicorns," said Raphaela. "They're calling us back."

The unicorns pricked up their ears and neighed back to their friends joyfully. Before Evie and Sparkles knew it, Diamond and the other unicorns were racing over the snarling black clouds back to the Stables. Soon, they were in view.

"We've made it!" cheered Wanda.
Raphaela led Evie, Juno, Wanda
and Storm into the stable yard just
as the first flash of lightning lit up
the clouds beneath them, making the
clouds shudder. All the other unicorns
and riders welcomed the rescue party
back, relieved and happy to be together
again. Professor Nimbus and Madam
Mariposa were standing at the front.
As soon as they dismounted, Professor
Nimbus rushed up to Storm.

"I'm so glad you're safe," she said,
giving her niece a big hug. "I've been
so worried."

"I'm all right," replied Storm,
"thanks to Misty. You should have
seen her jump. She was amazing!"

"Well, maybe you'll make the
Olympic team after all!" said Professor

Nimbus, stroking Misty's mane.

Storm told her aunt all about how she and Misty had been stranded on the cloud island. While she listened to her niece, Professor Nimbus glared at Raphaela.

"Please don't be angry with Raphaela," said Storm, as Raphaela led Galaxy to her stable. "I wouldn't have been able to get off that cloud without her help."

"Don't you worry yourself," said Professor Nimbus. "Just settle your unicorn in and then come to the Great Hall. I'm sure you and your friends need some cake after all that excitement."

All the cloud sprites had fed and settled their unicorns so Professor Nimbus took them to the Great Hall for tea. Juno, Wanda, Storm and Evie took off their unicorn's tack, brushed out their coats and helped them to recover from their adventure with a gentle massage. The unicorns settled quickly and enjoyed the fresh

water and hay that Skye and Madam
Mariposa brought them.

"Well done for today," said Evie to
Storm. "I could never have jumped
over that gap. You and Misty are an
amazing team."

"She's the best unicorn ever," said
Storm, giving Misty a gentle hug.

"Your aunt seemed very proud of the way you rode today," said Madam Mariposa as she helped Storm brush out Misty's mane.

"I never thought my riding would be good enough for her," said Storm.

"Is that why you wanted a different unicorn?" asked Evie.

Storm looked embarrassed.

"I'm sorry, Misty," she said. "I thought you weren't as good as the other unicorns but today I realised that it was me that was stopping us from being a team. I wouldn't bond with you so you couldn't trust me."

"Trust is the key," said Madam Mariposa. "You learnt that just in time and it saved you and your unicorn from being lost in the sky."

"I'll never forget it," promised Storm. "It's not about being the boss like my aunt said, it's about getting to know each other, listening to each other and being the best team you can be."

"That sounds like good advice," said Skye. "Not just for riders and their unicorns, but for friends too."

Storm smiled at them all and then took Wanda's hand.

"I know it won't make up for what I did," she said, "but I'm so sorry about the way I've treated you and Zephyr. I won't ever make the same mistake again."

"I'm so glad you're bonding with Misty," said Wanda. "You make a great team."

"I think we all make a great team," said Evie. And everyone cheered.

CHAPTER 7
Team Cloud Sprite

When all the unicorns were settled,
Sparkles led Evie, Juno, Wanda and
Madam Mariposa to the dining room.
As they followed the path, Madam
Mariposa told them something about
Raphaela and Professor Nimbus.

"Your aunt used to love coming
to Unicorn Riding Camp years ago,"
she said. "It was here that she met
Raphaela and they became best friends.
But after a few years, they had to
compete for a place in the Olympic
team. Raphaela beat your aunt by a

whisker in the finals and Professor Nimbus never got over it or forgave her old friend."

"That's so sad. I wonder if they'll ever be able to be friends again," said Storm as they walked into the dining room. "I hope so, after all, Raphaela helped me to bond with Misty!"

"It looks like they might have started," said Wanda.

She was right; Professor Nimbus and Raphaela were sharing a pot of tea.

They had a lot of catching up to do.

The friends sat down at their table, which was full of the most divine-looking cakes.

"All this adventure has given me the most enormous appetite!" laughed Juno, as they all tucked in.

Evie's favourites were the cloudberry puffs. They were sprinkled with tiny rain crystals that exploded in her mouth!

"Well Evie," said Skye. "I know I

said that Unicorn Riding Camp would be fun, but I didn't think for a minute that it would be quite so exciting!"

"I don't think any of us will be awake for the midnight feast tonight," said Wanda. "I'm exhausted."

"Can you stay Evie?" asked Storm.

"I'd love to," said Evie, "but we really have to get back so that I can settle all my ponies for the night."

"You must come for the next Riding Camp now that you're part of our team," said Wanda.

The friends all agreed that Evie, Diamond and, of course, Sparkles would always be welcome. Then they got up to help Evie prepare for the ride home. Professor Nimbus and Raphaela got up to say goodbye.

"Thank you for coming to our

camp," said Raphaela. "You've been a great team player."

"Who knows," added Professor Nimbus, "if you keep training at Unicorn Riding Camp, you may be selected for the Olympic team one day!"

When they got to the stables, Evie could see that her unicorn was tired from the day's adventures.

"Don't worry, Diamond," said Evie. "We'll soon be home. But first we have to say goodbye to all our friends."

The unicorns whickered and touched noses saying their unicorn goodbyes.

"We'll see you all soon!" said Evie. as she mounted Diamond using the technique Raphaela had taught them. "Hope you all have fun at camp tomorrow!"

"We will!" smiled Wanda.

The thunderstorm was over and the sunset clouds had begun to glow with warm pinks. As soon as Diamond trotted out through the golden gate, Evie and Sparkles spotted the tunnel of trees.

When they arrived at Starlight Stables, the sun was setting behind the Golden Mountain and the clouds burned with pinks, reds and magentas. There, waiting beside Diamond's stable door, was Diamond's kit. A riding jacket was folded neatly on top of the brushes.

"It's a unicorn rider's jacket for the Olympic team," said Evie, as she tried it on.

It didn't fit her at all, it was far too big. Evie tried to hide her disappointment and Sparkles comforted her with a purr.

"Of course, Sparkles," smiled Evie. "This isn't for me to wear now. It's for when I'm ready for the team – when I'm older and I've perfected all the skills an Olympic rider needs."

Evie hugged her beautiful new riding jacket.

"Thank you cloud sprites," she said, "and thank you Diamond. What a very special unicorn!"

"Miaow!" said Sparkles, as he chased a tiny pink cloudlet that floated across the yard.

Pony Facts
&
Activities

Evie

LIVES AT:
Starlight Stables

FAVOURITE FOOD:
Apple blossom ice cream

FAVOURITE PASTIME:
Going on adventures
with my magic ponies

FAVOURITE FLOWER:
Violets

FANTASY JOB:
Training unicorns
for the Olympics

Diamond

BREED:
Connemara pony

FEATURES:
Very strong and very good jumpers

HEIGHT:
Up to 14 hands

COLOUR:
Grey is the most popular colour
but they can be black, bay,
brown, dun, roan and chestnut.

Step-by-step

Evie goes to riding camp to learn how to be an even better rider. Can you put these steps to riding a pony into the right order? Write the order from 1 to 7 in the circles. Once you've done this then put the other pony facts in order.

A.

Getting your horse ready to ride

◯ Check the saddle is on securely.

◯ Put the bridle on.

◯ Check your pony is calm and has no injuries.

◯ Mount your pony.

◯ Put the saddle on.

◯ Put your foot in the stirrup.

◯ Make sure your riding hat is on securely.

B.

After a ride

◯ Take off the saddle.

◯ Loosen the saddle slightly.

◯ Take off the bridle.

◯ Walk the horse around until it is cool.

◯ Comb where the saddle was.

◯ Put your pony back in its stable or pasture.

C.

The speeds of a horse

◯ Gallop.

◯ Trot.

◯ Halt.

◯ Walk.

◯ Canter.

Unicorn Facts

Unicorns have appeared in many stories throughout history. The descriptions of them have varied – some are described as ponylike, white with golden horns, others as more goatlike! The word unicorn means single horn, and all unicorns in history have had this in common. Unicorns are supposed to have great powers but are very hard to catch. and narwhals.

Their tears and blood are supposed
to have healing powers. For this reason
there have always been people trying
to catch them. Unicorns are mentioned
in many historical texts but a lot
of these authors could actually be
confusing them with rhinoceroses,
white deers and narwhals.

Scrambles

Can you unscramble these pony words?

Check your answers at the bottom of the page.

1. aerm

2. olaf

3. adleds

4. irens

5. fhoo

6. stpareu

7. bletsa

8. phrsdujo

9. nypo

10. ital

Fantasy Job

Evie had such fun at the unicorn riding camp,
she'd love to compete in the Unicorn Olympics
one day. What would be your fantasy job?

....
....
....
....
....
....
....
....
....
....
....
....
....
....
....
....
....
....

Crossword

Can you fill in this crossword by answering
the questions below?

Across:

3. Where Evie keeps her special things

5. Zephyr's owner

6. Stables where Evie's ponies live

Down:

1. Evie's Unicorn

2. The type of pony Diamond is

3. The unicorn empathy teacher

4. The name for horse's equipment

6. Evie's friend at camp

7. A pony's foot

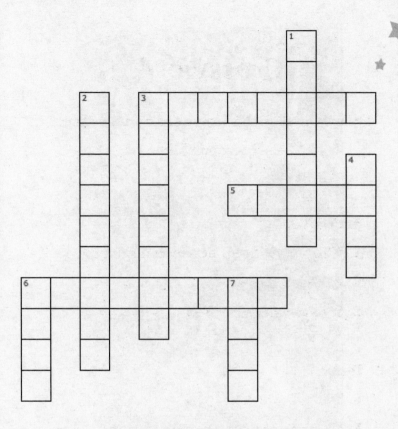

Look out for more
of Princess Evie's
magical adventures at a
bookshop near you!